Dick Whittington and his cat

and other stories

First published in 2002 by Miles Kelly Publishing,
Bardfield Centre, Great Bardfield, Essex CM7 4SL

24681097531

Copyright © Miles Kelly Publishing Ltd 2002

Project manager: Paula Borton
Editorial Assistant: Nicola Sail

British Library Cataloguing-in-Publication Data
A catalogue record for this book is available from the British Library

ISBN 1-84236-090-6

Printed in Hong Kong

Visit us on the web:
www.mileskelly.net
Info@mileskelly.net

Dick Whittington and his cat

and other stories

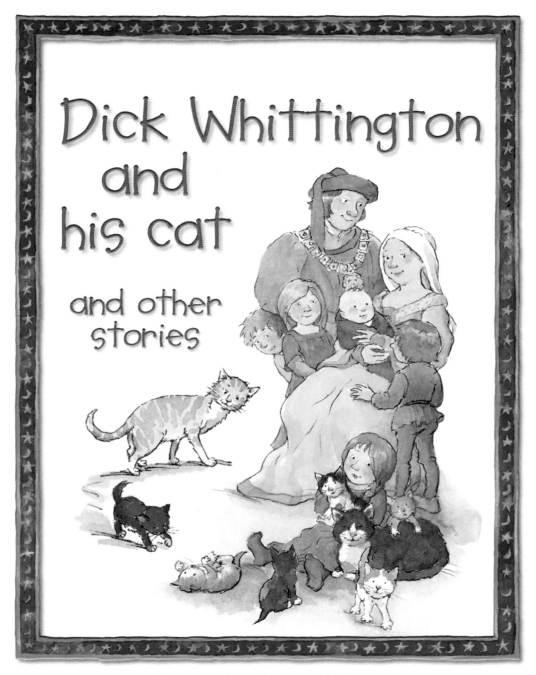

Chosen by Fiona Waters

Miles Kelly
PUBLISHING

Contents

Sleeping Beauty

a retelling from the original tale by Charles Perrault

Long, long ago, when fairies were still able to grant wishes, there lived a king and queen who wanted, more than anything in the whole world, to have a baby daughter. When their wish was finally granted and a beautiful tiny princess lay in her cradle, the king and queen decided to have a great candlelit party to celebrate. They invited the twelve most important fairies in the land and a great many other people besides.

As well as the thousands of glittering candles, there were golden tables piled high with all kinds of delicious food, and the royal orchestra played their most cheerful tunes. The twelve fairies all lined up to present their christening gifts to the tiny princess. Their gifts were those that only a fairy can give: beauty, kindness, grace, honesty and the like. The princess smiled happily in her cradle as one by one the fairies tiptoed up.

The eleventh fairy had just promised the princess a sweet singing voice, when there was a great roll of thunder and all the candles flickered out. There stood quite the most wicked fairy anyone had ever seen. She was dressed all in black, her long straggly hair was black and her eyes, glittering in rage, were as black as the crow's feathers. Her voice was like a saw as she screeched, "How dare you not invite me to the party! I too have a gift for the little princess," and she smiled a not very nice smile. "Because you have forgotten me, my gift is that when the princess is sixteen she shall prick her finger on a spindle and die!" and with a horrid laugh, the wicked fairy disappeared with another clap of thunder.

As the candles were hastily relit, everyone started talking at once. Then a quiet voice was heard over all the hubbub. It was the twelfth fairy.

"I cannot undo this wicked spell," she whispered, "but I can decree that the princess will not die. She will instead fall into a deep sleep for a hundred years," and all the fairies slipped away leaving the court in despair.

The king, of course, immediately ordered that all the spinning wheels in the land were to be burned. After a while, everyone grew less frightened, and as the princess grew up into the most lovely girl, the wicked fairy's prediction slipped from most people's memories.

On her sixteenth birthday the princess went exploring. At the top of a tower she did not remember seeing before, she found an old woman, sitting at a spinning wheel.

It was, of course, the wicked fairy in disguise. The princess was fascinated and, as she bent forward to look at the cloth, her hand caught the sharp spindle and she immediately fell to the ground as though dead. With a swirl of smoke and a nasty laugh, the wicked fairy disappeared.

Everyone else in the palace fell asleep at the same moment. The king fell asleep with his ministers, the queen and her maids fell asleep in her dressing room. The cook fell asleep in the kitchen in the middle of baking a cake, the groom fell asleep as he fed the horses in the stables and even the little linnet the princess had in a golden cage by her bedside fell asleep on its perch. A great high thorn hedge grew up and soon the palace was completely hidden. Time stood still and all was silent.

Many, many years passed. The tale of the sleeping princess spread far and wide, and many came to try to find her. But no one could get through the thorn hedge. And so after even more years, people forgot what lay behind the hedge.

Then one day a handsome prince came riding through the woods, and as he reached the thorn hedge, thousands of pink roses burst into bloom. The prince walked forward, and a path appeared leading through the hedge towards the palace. It was a hundred years to the day since the princess had pricked her finger. The prince was astonished by the sight that met his eyes. Everywhere people lay asleep, frozen in the midst of whatever they had been doing when the spell caught them.

The prince climbed the tower, and there he found the princess, looking as lovely as ever. He bent over and kissed her, and immediately the spell was broken. The king and his ministers carried on just where they had left off. The queen chose which dress she wanted to wear and the maids brushed her hair. The cook put her cake in the oven and the

groom led the horses out into the courtyard. And even the little linnet in her golden cage sang a joyful song.

As for the princess. . . ! Well, she and the prince had fallen in love with each other on the spot, and were married the very next day. They all lived happily ever after, and the wicked fairy was never ever seen again.

The Three Little Pigs

an English folk tale

There once was a mother pig who had three little pigs. They were very poor indeed, and the day came when the mother pig could no longer look after the family. She sent the three little pigs out into the wide world to seek their fortunes.

The first little pig met a man carrying a big bundle of straw.

"Oh, please may I have that bundle of straw to build myself a house?" asked the first little pig. The man was tired of carrying the bundle of straw so he gladly gave it to the first little pig.

The first little pig built a very fine house out of the bundle of straw, and he lived there very happily. Then along came a big bad wolf.

"Little pig, little pig, let me come in!" shouted the wolf.

"No, no, not by the hair on my chinny chin chin. I'll not let you in," squeaked the first little pig.

"Then I'll huff and I'll puff, and I'll blow your house down," yelled the wolf. And he did. He huffed and he puffed and he blew the straw house down. The first little pig ran away as fast as his trotters would carry him.

Now the second little pig met a man carrying a bundle of sticks.

"Oh, please may I have that bundle of sticks to build myself a house?" asked the second little pig. The man was tired of carrying the bundle of sticks so he gladly gave it to the second little pig.

The second little pig built a very fine house out of the bundle of sticks, and he lived there very happily. Then along came the big bad wolf.

"Little pig, little pig, let me come in!" shouted the wolf.

"No, no, not by the hair on my chinny chin chin. I'll not let you in," squeaked the second little pig.

"Then I'll huff and I'll puff, and I'll blow your house down," yelled the wolf. And he did. He huffed and he puffed and he blew the stick house down. The second little pig ran away as fast as his trotters would carry him.

Now the third little pig met a man carrying a big load of bricks.

"Oh, please may I have that load of bricks to build myself a house?" asked the third little pig. The man was very tired indeed from carrying the big load of bricks so he gladly gave it to the third little pig.

The third little pig built a very fine house out of the big load of bricks, and he lived there very happily. Then along came the big bad wolf.

"Little pig, little pig, let me come in!" shouted the wolf.

"No, no, not by the hair on my chinny chin chin. I'll not let you in," squeaked the third little pig.

"Then I'll huff and I'll puff, and I'll blow your house down," yelled the wolf. And he tried. He huffed and he puffed but he could not blow the brick house down.

"Little pig, little pig, I am coming down your chimney to get you," bellowed the wolf.

"Please yourself," called the third little pig who was busy with some preparations of his own.

"Little pig, little pig, I have my front paws down your chimney," threatened the wolf.

"Please yourself," called the third little pig who was still

busy with some
preparations of his own.

"Little pig, little pig,
I have my great
bushy tail down your
chimney," called
the wolf.

"Please yourself,"
called the third little
pig who was now
sitting in his rocking
chair by the fireside.

"Little pig, little
pig, here I come!"
and with a great rush
and a huge SPLOSH!
the big bad wolf fell
right into the big pot
of boiling water that
the clever little pig had
placed on the fire, right under the
chimney. The wolf scrabbled and splashed and scrambled
out of the big pot and ran as fast as ever he could right out
of the front door. And he was never seen again. The third
little pig managed to find his two brothers, and they went
and fetched their mother. And they are all still living
happily together in the little brick house.

Snow White and Rose Red

a retelling from the original story by the Brothers Grimm

Once upon a time there was a widow who had two daughters, Snow White and Rose Red. Snow White was quiet and gentle, Rose Red was wild as the hills, but they loved each other, and their mother, so the little house in the woods was a happy one.

One winter's evening as they all sat round the fire there was a knock at the door. Rose Red opened it and gave a scream. There stood a great big brown bear! But in a deep rumbly voice the bear said,

"Please do not be afraid. All I ask is that you let me sleep by your fire tonight. It is so cold outside."

"Of course you may shelter with us," said the mother. And she called the girls to set the soup on the stove and to put another log on the fire.

"Would you brush the snow from my fur, please?" asked the bear. Rose Red fetched the big broom and carefully brushed the bear's great shaggy coat. Snow White gave him a great bowl of hot soup and the bear gulped it down in one. Then he stretched out in front of the fire and was soon fast asleep.

In the morning Snow White let him out of the cottage and he padded off into the forest through the deep snow. But in the evening, he returned and once again Snow White and Rose Red and their mother looked after him. After that the bear came every night all through the winter, and they all grew very fond of him. But when spring came, the bear told them he would not be returning any more.

"I have to guard my treasure. Once the snows have

melted all kinds of wicked people try to steal it," he said and giving them all a hug he set off through the forest. Just as he passed through the garden gate, his fur caught on a nail. For a fleeting moment Snow White thought she saw a glint of gold, but the bear hurried off and was soon out of sight.

A few days later, Rose Red and Snow White were out gathering berries to make jam when they came alongside a fallen tree. Then they saw a very cross dwarf, tugging at his beard which was trapped by the great tree trunk.

"Well, don't stand there like a pair of silly geese! Come and help me!" he shrieked.

Well, no matter how hard they tugged Rose Red and Snow White were not strong enough to lift the tree, so Rose Red took her scissors out and snipped off the end of the dwarf's beard. He was absolutely furious, and snatched up a big bag of gold from the tree roots and disappeared without a word of thanks.

Some days later the girls' mother said she really fancied a piece of fish for supper, so they went down to the river to see what they could catch. But instead of a fish, there on the bank they found their friend the cross dwarf again. This time his beard was all caught up in his fishing line.

"Don't just stand there gawping," he yelled, "help me get free!"

Snow White tried to untangle it but it was impossible so she too snipped a piece off his beard. He was quite white with rage, but just grasped a casket of jewels that lay at the water's edge and turned away without a word of thanks.

It was the Spring Fair a few days later. The girls decided to go and buy some new ribbons for their hats, and their mother wanted needles for her embroidery, so they set off early in the morning. They had not gone far when they heard a terrible shrieking and crying. They ran towards the sound, and there once more was the cross dwarf, this time struggling in the huge talons of an eagle. They tugged and tugged and the eagle had to let go.

"You have torn my coat," muttered the ungrateful dwarf and picked up a basket of pearls and hobbled off as fast as possible. The girls just laughed and continued on their way to the fair.

They had a wonderful time, and it was quite late when they walked slowly home. The sun was just sinking behind a big rock when, to their astonishment, they came across the dwarf again. There spread out on the ground in front of him was a great pile of gold and precious jewels and pearls.

Suddenly the dwarf saw Snow White and Rose Red.

"Go away! Go away! You horrid girls are always in my way," he shouted. But just then there was a huge growl and the great brown bear stood by their side. With one huge paw he swiped the dwarf up, up into the sky and no one ever saw where he fell to

earth again. The bear turned towards
Snow White and Rose Red and as they
looked, his great shaggy coat fell away.
There stood a handsome young man, dressed
in a golden suit of the richest velvet.

"Do not be afraid, Snow White and Rose
Red," he said smiling. "Now you can see who I really
am. That wicked dwarf put a spell on me so he could steal
all my treasure, but you have broken the spell by
your kindness."

They all went home, laden with the treasure. They
talked long into the night, and it was all still true the next

morning! Snow White
married the handsome
young man who, by
great good fortune,
had a younger
brother who
married Rose
Red, so they all
lived happily
ever after.

But if you
ever find a dwarf
with half his beard
missing, I would be very
careful if I were you.

The Giant who Counted Carrots

a German fairytale

High upon a mountainside there was once a giant who was always very sleepy, and when he went to sleep, he would sleep for hundreds of years at a time. So every time he awoke things had changed a great deal. He spent time as a herdsman, but he did not like being poor. So he went back to sleep. On another visit he spent time as a rich farmer but he found his servants cheated him so he went back to sleep. When he eventually awoke again he wandered down the mountainside to see what he could see.

He came upon a rock pool where a waterfall tumbled down the rocks. A group of laughing girls were sitting dangling their toes in the water. The giant hid and watched. One of the girls was quieter than the others, but to the giant she was the prettiest. Her name was Elizabeth and she was to be married in a few days to the young duke. She and her friends chattered about the forthcoming celebrations as they paddled in the pool, and all the while the giant watched. When they skipped away, his heart grew sad. He realised just how very lonely he was.

He decided to try to win Elizabeth's heart. All through the night he worked. He covered the steep stone under the waterfall with white marble so it sparkled in the clear water. He lined the pool with silver, and filled it with darting golden fish. He covered the banks with rich green grass, planted with sweetly-smelling violets and forget-me-nots and deep blue hyacinths. Then he hid himself again.

25

When the girls arrived they were astonished, but Elizabeth looked thoughtful. She knew that some powerful enchantment had been at work. She wandered to the edge and looked deep into the silver pool, full of the golden fish. And as she looked she heard a voice, whispering, whispering to her to step into the pool. There was a sudden splash, and as her friends looked round in alarm, Elizabeth slipped into the pool. The girls ran over to the pool and looked into the silver depths. In vain they tried to find her. When they went home and told the young duke, he came with all haste to the pool. All the giant's adornments had vanished. The waterfall fell over steep and black rocks, the silver lining and the golden fish had disappeared from the pool, and there was not a single flower to be seen. Sadly, the duke went back to the palace and nothing would cheer him.

Meanwhile Elizabeth found herself in the giant's garden. He begged her to stay with him and be his queen, but she told him she loved the duke and would not forsake him. The giant hoped she would forget the duke, but as the

days passed he saw that she grew pale and sad. He
wondered how he could cheer her, and change her mind.
Then he remembered his magic staff. Whatever it touched
would turn into any animal he wished for. He gave the staff
to Elizabeth and for a few hours she was happy as,
first a kitten then a dog then a canary appeared
thanks to the staff. But it was not long before
she grew silent again.

    Now the giant grew very good
carrots, and he was very proud of
his carrots. He pulled some for
supper and Elizabeth said she
had never tasted such
delicious carrots in all her life,
which was true.
So the next day, the giant took
Elizabeth out into the fields
round the castle where the carrots
grew. As far as the eye could see
there were carrots, row upon row
of them. Elizabeth asked the giant
how many there were, but he
couldn't tell her that at all. So she
begged him to count at least one
row, and as he began counting she quickly drew the staff
out from under her cloak and touched a black stone that
lay on the ground. It turned into a black horse with great

hooves that pounded the earth as Elizabeth mounted its back and fled down the valley away, away from the giant.

The very next day, Elizabeth married her duke and they lived happily ever after. The lonely giant went slowly back to his garden, and fell into a deep sleep. Many hundreds of years passed and still the giant never awoke. In time grass and plants and trees grew over the slumbering giant, and still he slept on. Over the years the mound that was the sleeping giant became known as Giant Mountain, and so it is still called today. So beware if you see great rows of carrots on a mountain side, you might be very near a sleeping giant!

Dick Whittington and his Cat

an English myth

Hundreds of years ago there lived a poor orphan boy called Dick Whittington. His only possession was his cat, but everyone in his village looked after him, so he never wanted for a meal or clothes on his back. In return, he worked hard wherever he was needed. Now Dick's greatest dream was to visit the great city of London where, he had heard, the streets were paved with gold.

One day, a waggoner pulled into the village to give his two great shire horses a drink. Dick offered to rub the horses down, and before long he was telling the waggoner all about his dreams of visiting London town.

"Well, you must be in luck today," smiled the waggoner, "for that is where I am bound. Why don't you come with me and I will drop you off back here again when I return tomorrow?"

This was too good
an offer to refuse, so Dick
and his cat waved
goodbye to the villagers
and set off with the
waggoner for London.
When they arrived, Dick
looked round about in
astonishment. Never
before had he seen such
huge buildings, all
crowded so closely
together. And there were
so many people! Dick
set off to explore,
promising the waggoner

he would be back in the evening.

The pavements certainly did not appear to be made of
gold. But he kept on thinking he should just try round the
next corner, and then the next and, before long, Dick
realised that he was hopelessly lost. He stumbled into a
doorway, and worn out with hunger and worry at not
keeping his promise to help the waggoner, he fell fast asleep.

Now as luck would have it, Dick had chosen a very
good doorway to sleep in. The house belonged to a rich
merchant, Mr Fitzwarren, who was very kind and always
willing to help anyone in need. So when he came home

later that evening, Mr Fitzwarren took Dick and his cat indoors and told the cook to give him supper. The cook was very grumpy indeed at having to prepare a meal late at night for Dick who, she thought, looked like a ragamuffin.

The next morning, Dick told Mr Fitzwarren the whole story. Smiling, Mr Fitzwarren told Dick that, as he had found, the streets of London were not paved with gold, and indeed life there was very hard.

"But you look like a strong boy, would you like to work for me, Dick?" he asked. "You will have a roof over your head and a good dinner every day in return for helping in the kitchen and the stables."

Dick was delighted, and he soon settled into the household. He worked hard, and everyone liked him, except the cook. She gave him all the really horrible jobs in the kitchen and would never let him have a moment's rest. But she didn't dare defy her master and so Dick had his good dinner every day.

Now whenever one of Mr Fitzwarren's ships went to sea, it was his custom to ask everyone in the household to give something to the ship's cargo for luck. Poor Dick had only his cat and it was with a very heavy heart that he handed her over.

The ship was at sea for many, many months before they finally came to port in China. The captain and the crew went ashore to show the emperor the cargo they had brought all the way from London. The emperor had known the captain for many years and they were old friends, so they sat down to a state banquet before discussing business. But to the emperor's great embarrassment, the entire meal was ruined by the rats that boldly ran everywhere, even over the plates they were eating off. The emperor explained that they had tried everything but nothing could rid the court of the plague of rats. The captain smiled.

"I think I have the answer," he said and he sent for Dick's cat. Within moments of her arrival, there were piles of dead rats at the emperor's feet. He was so impressed that he gave the captain a ship full of gold just for the cat.

Back in London, Dick's life was a misery. The cook was nastier than ever and he didn't even have his beloved cat for company, so one day he ran away, intending to walk home to his village. But he had not gone far before he heard the church bells ringing, and they seemed to say,

"Turn again Dick Wittington,
Thrice Lord Mayor of London."
Dick didn't know what the bells
meant, but he remembered how
kind Mr Fitzwarren had been, so
he turned round again and
went back before the cook
had even noticed that he
was missing. Of course
when the ships came home,
Mr Fitzwarren gave Dick his
fair share and more. This was the
start of Dick's prosperity, and he
even married Mr Fitzwarren's
daughter, Jane. He did become
Lord Mayor of London three
times, but he never forgot
his early days of
poverty and he founded
schools and hospitals for
the poor. He and
Jane had many
children, and
there were
always lots of
cats in their great
house as well!

The Ugly Duckling

a retelling from the original story by Hans Christian Andersen

The mother duck was waiting for her eggs to hatch. Slowly the first shell cracked and first a tiny bill and then a little yellow wing appeared. Then with a great rush, a bedraggled yellow duckling fell out. He stretched his wings and began to clean his feathers. Soon he stood proudly beside his mother, watching as his sisters and brothers all pushed their way out of their shells.

There was only one shell left. It was the largest, and the mother duck wondered why it was taking so much longer than the others. She wanted to take her babies down to the river for their first swimming lesson. There was a sudden loud crack, and there lay quite the biggest and ugliest duckling she had ever seen. He wasn't even yellow. His feathers were dull brown and grey.

"Oh dear," said the mother duck.

She led the family down to the river, the ugly duckling trailing along behind the others. They all splashed into the water, and were soon swimming gracefully, all except the ugly duckling who looked large and ungainly even on the water.

"Oh dear," said the mother duck.

The whole family set off for the farmyard where they were greeted with hoots and moos and barks and snorts from all the other animals.

"Whatever is that?" said the rooster, pointing rudely at the ugly duckling. All the other ducklings huddled round their mother and tried to pretend the ugly duckling was not with them.

"Oh dear," said the mother duck.

The ugly duckling felt very sad and lonely. No one seemed to like him, so he ran away from the farmyard and

hid in some dark reeds by the
river. Some hunters came
by with their loud noisy
guns and big fierce dogs.
The ugly duckling
paddled deeper
into the reeds,
trembling with
fear. Only later
in the day, as it
was growing
dark, did the
ugly duckling
dare move from
his hiding place.

All summer he
wandered over fields and
down rivers. Everywhere he went people
laughed and jeered at him, and all the other ducks he met
just hissed at him or tried to bite his tail. As well as being
ugly, the duckling was very lonely and unhappy. Soon
winter came and the rivers began to freeze over. One day
the duckling found himself trapped in the ice. He tucked his
head under his wing, and decided that his short life must
have come to an end.

He was still there early the next morning when a
farmer came by on his way to feed the cows in the fields.

The farmer broke the ice with his shoe, and wrapped the ugly duckling in his jacket then carried him home to his children. They put the poor frozen ugly duckling in a box by the fire, and as he thawed out they fed him and stroked his feathers. And there the ugly duckling stayed through the winter, growing bigger all the time.

Now the farmer's wife had never had much time for the ugly duckling. He was always getting under her feet in the kitchen, and he was so clumsy that he kept knocking things over. He spilt the milk in the bucket from the cow. He put his great feet in the freshly churned butter. He was just a nuisance, and one day the farmer's wife had enough. So, in a rage, she chased him out of her kitchen, out of the farmyard and through the gate down the lane.

It was a perfect spring day. The apple trees were covered in blossom, the grass was green and the air was filled with the sound of birdsong. The ugly duckling wandered down to the river, and there he saw three magnificent pure white swans. They were beautiful and so graceful as they glided over towards the bank where he stood. He waited for them to hiss at him and beat the water with their great wings to frighten him away, but they didn't do any such thing. Instead they called him to come and join them. At first he thought it was a joke, but they asked him again.

He bent down to get into the water, and there looking back at him was his own reflection. But where was the ugly duckling? All he could see was another great and magnificent swan. He was a swan! Not an ugly duckling but a swan. He lifted his great long elegant neck, and called in sheer delight, "I am a swan! I am a SWAN!" and he sailed gracefully over the water to join his real family.

The Mermaid of Zennor

a Cornish legend

The bell was ringing, calling the villagers of Zennor to Sunday service. It was a simple little granite towered church, built to withstand the wild winds and weather that could roll in from the sea. Matthew Trewella stood in the choir stalls and looked at the new bench he had been carving. It was nearly finished and wanted only one more panel to be carved.

As the voices of the congregation rang out in the hymns, a sweet pure voice was heard. A voice that no one had heard before. When the villagers turned to leave at the end of the service, there at the back of the little church stood the most beautiful woman any of them had ever seen. Her dress was made of soft rustling silk, at one moment green, the next blue, like the sea. Round her neck she wore a gleaming necklace of pearls, and her golden hair fell down her back almost to the floor.

As Matthew walked out, the woman placed her hand on his sleeve.

"Your carving is beautiful, Matthew."

Matthew blushed and turned his rough cap round and round in his great red hands, his deep blue eyes wary.

"Why, thank you ma'am," he managed to stutter before he fled out of the church. Where the beautiful lady went no one quite saw.

The next day Matthew was hard at work, carving the decoration of leaves that went round the edge of the bench when he heard the soft rustle of silk. There stood the woman again.

"What will you put in the last panel, Matthew?" she whispered. And she smiled into his deep blue eyes. Matthew sensed a strong smell of the sea in the tiny church as he bent to get up off his knees but when he looked up again, there was no sign of the woman.

The next Sunday the lady was in church again. She looked deep into Matthew's eyes as she sang the hymns, and when he walked slowly out, as if in a dream, she was waiting for him.

"Will you carve my image in the last panel, Matthew?" she asked and her voice was gentle and sighing like the

withdrawing tide on a shingle beach. Matthew's deep blue
eyes gazed far over her head, out towards the sea, but he did
not reply. Only the schoolmaster and his wife noticed that
the seat where the woman had sat was wet, wet with sea
water. But they said nothing.

Time passed, and every Sunday the woman came to
church. Matthew seemed like
a man in a dream, his
eyes always looking
out to sea. The
final panel was
still not finished
on the bench.
November came,
and with it the
mist curled up
from the sea.
Night after
night a light was
to be seen late in
the church. The
gentle sound of
wood chipping
drifted out with the
mist, but no one
ventured into the church.

It was the parson who

discovered the finished bench when he went in to open up the church one morning. The church floor was wet, wet with sea water. The stub of a candle stood among a great pile of wood shavings on the floor. The final panel of the bench was the best Matthew had ever carved. It was a mermaid, long hair falling down her back, the scales of her great fish tail in deep relief. She looked almost alive.

Matthew Trewella had not slept in his bed that night, nor was he ever seen again in Zennor. The mysterious woman never came to church again. The schoolmaster and his wife never talked of the wet seat. Only the fishermen would shake their heads as they sat talking on the winter's evenings. They would talk of the mermaid they had seen off the coast, and of the young man with the deep blue eyes who was always swimming by her side.

Cinderella

a retelling from the original tale by Charles Perrault

Once upon a time, when there were still fairy godmothers, there was a girl called Cinderella. She lived with her father and his new wife, and her two new step-sisters. The step-mother did not like Cinderella very much, mostly because she was so much nicer than her own two daughters. Cinderella was also much prettier. Oh, but the step-sisters were ugly!

Cinderella had to do all the work in the house as the ugly sisters were also very lazy. They spent all the father's money on new clothes and endless pairs of shoes, and then went off to parties leaving poor Cinderella with piles of stockings to mend.

One day a very grand invitation arrived. The prince was looking for a wife, and had decided to give a ball in three days time for all the young ladies in the land. The ugly sisters could talk about nothing else. They bought lots

of new dresses and many pairs
of matching shoes, and
then spent every hour
trying them all on. They
made Cinderella curl their
hair and iron their ribbons
and powder their noses.
Cinderella was so
exhausted running
around after them
that she had no time
to look into her own
wardrobe to choose
what she should wear.

In a waft of perfume,
the ugly sisters swept out
of the door into the carriage
without as much as a thank you to
Cinderella. She closed the door sadly, and went to sit by the
fire in the kitchen.

"I do wish I could have gone to the ball, too," she
sighed.

There was a sudden swirl of silver stars, and there in
front of Cinderella stood an old lady with a twinkle in her
eye, and a wand in her hand.

"You shall go to the ball, my dear Cinderella. I am
your fairy godmother," she said, smiling at Cinderella.

"Now, we must be quick, there is much to do! Please bring me a large pumpkin from the vegetable patch. Oh, and six mice from the barn, and you will find four lizards by the water butt."

Cinderella did as she was bid. With a wave of the wand,

the pumpkin was turned into a glittering golden coach and the mice into six pure white horses. The lizards became elegant footmen, dressed in green velvet.

"Now you, my dear," said the fairy godmother, turning to Cinderella. A wave of the wand, and Cinderella's old apron disappeared and there she stood in a white dress, glittering with golden stars. Her hair was piled on top of her head and it too was sprinkled with stars. On her feet were tiny glass slippers with diamonds sparkling in the heels.

"Enjoy yourself, my dear," said the fairy godmother, "but you must leave before midnight for then my magic ends and you will be back in your old apron with some mice and lizards at your feet!"

When Cinderella arrived at the ball everyone turned to look at this unknown beauty who had arrived so unexpectedly. The prince hurried over to ask her to dance and then would not dance with anyone else all evening. The ugly sisters were beside themselves with rage, which of course made them look even uglier.

Cinderella was enjoying herself so much that she forgot the fairy godmother's warning, so she had a terrible fright when the clock began to strike midnight. She turned from the prince with a cry and ran down the stairs of the palace into her carriage, and disappeared as suddenly as she had arrived. One of the tiny glass slippers with diamonds sparkling in the heels had slipped from her foot as she ran. The prince picked it up and turning to the crowded ballroom declared, "I shall marry the girl whose foot fits this slipper!"

Cinderella, meanwhile, had just managed to reach her garden gate when all her finery disappeared, and by the time the ugly sisters arrived home, both in a towering rage, she was sitting quietly by the fire.

The next morning, the prince went from house to house looking for the mystery girl whose foot would fit the tiny glass slipper. But no one had feet that small. He reached Cinderella's house where first one ugly sister and then the next tried to squash their huge feet into the slipper.

"Please let me try," said a quiet voice from the corner, and Cinderella stepped forward. The sisters just laughed in scorn but they soon stopped when they saw that the tiny slipper fitted Cinderella perfectly. There was a sudden swirl of silver stars, and there in front of Cinderella stood her fairy godmother with a twinkle in her eye, and a wand

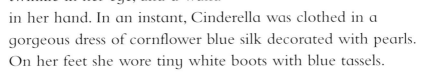

in her hand. In an instant, Cinderella was clothed in a gorgeous dress of cornflower blue silk decorated with pearls. On her feet she wore tiny white boots with blue tassels.

The prince whisked Cinderella off to the palace to meet the king and queen, and the wedding took place the very next day. Cinderella forgave the two ugly sisters, she was that sort of girl. But the prince insisted the sisters spent one day a week working in the palace kitchens just to remind them how horrid they had been to Cinderella.